To Brittany Xmas 1993

From Karen Anderson
(Brit the illustrations were done
By my cousin sue Ellen

To Brigann, Xmas 1993

From Karen Anderson

(but the illustrations were done by my cousin Sue Burns)

WINTER'S CHILD

WINTER'S CHILD

Mary K. Whittington

illustrated by Sue Ellen Brown

Atheneum ♦ 1992 ♦ New York

Maxwell Macmillan Canada

Toronto

Maxwell Macmillan International

New York   Oxford   Singapore   Sydney

Atheneum
Macmillan Publishing Company
866 Third Avenue
New York, NY 10022

Maxwell Macmillan Canada, Inc.
1200 Eglinton Avenue East
Suite 200
Don Mills, Ontario M3C 3N1

Macmillan Publishing Company is part of the Maxwell Communication
Group of Companies.

First edition
Printed in Hong Kong

10 9 8 7 6 5 4 3 2 1
The text of this book is set in Bernhard Modern.
The illustrations are rendered in acrylic and colored pencil.

LIBRARY OF CONGRESS CATALOGING-IN-PUBLICATION DATA
Whittington, Mary K.
Winter's child/Mary K. Whittington; illustrated by Sue Ellen
Brown.—1st ed.
p.   cm.
Summary: Winter discovers a child in the snow and takes her home
to raise as his daughter, only to find that she is Spring and will
take his place.
ISBN 0-689-31685-2
[1. Winter—Fiction. 2. Spring—Fiction. 3. Seasons—Fiction.]
I. Brown, Sue Ellen, ill. II. Title.
PZ7.W6188W1 1992
[E]—dc20   91-25011

To all my friends
in the Wednesday Morning Children's
Writers Group

M. K. W.

To Nancy Lewis,
for her unfailing support

S. E. B.

On a cold white morning, Winter whistles up his wolves.
Yipping with eagerness, they bound through the snow to frisk
about his feet, to lick his hands. His laughter echoes among the
trees as he romps with the wolves, then harnesses them to his sled
of glittering ice.

"Come, O North Wind, my only friend," he shouts, and rides into the forest. The frosty air rings with the music of silver bells on the traces, with the yelping of the running wolves.

At the top of a hill Winter reins in his team, for he sees a small bundle, half covered with snow, lying between the roots of a great hollow oak.

North Wind whips snow into clouds about Winter's boots.
"Let us go," she moans. But Winter strides to the bundle and
bends to brush away the snow. "A child," he says in wonder.

"Do not wake her," North Wind howls, "for she is Spring, who
will one day drive you away."

"No," Winter says, "she is but a babe, and all alone."
He gathers her up, holds her close. "I too am lonely."

Leaping back upon the sled, he turns the wolves homeward, to his house of white stone. When Spring awakens, shivering, he wraps her in soft woolen robes. When she cries with hunger, he gives her apple mush and maple sap to drink. He sings lullabies so he will not have to listen to North Wind rattling the windows and sighing at the door.

Spring grows. Never has Winter been so happy. Soon she follows him outside when he tends his garden of crystalline ice flowers.

She calls him Father and laughs when he showers her with snow, the flakes falling from his fingers.

Winter and Spring go on long sled rides. He teaches her to make snowballs and watches her slide on river ice. And Spring grows taller and more beautiful.

One morning North Wind whistles in Winter's ears. "Wake up. She has gone."

"I do not believe you," Winter answers.

But the door stands open, and a trail of footprints leads into the forest.

"Spring," he cries, stumbling from his bed. His voice cracks, his heart pounds harder with every step.

He finds her by a frozen pool at the river's edge. Before he can scold, she turns, smiling.

"See, Father, what I can do." She brushes her hand across the ice and it melts at her touch.

In the still water he sees his reflection, the wrinkled face of an old man.

Spring wraps her arms around a tree and laughs as snow on its branches melts and falls in a shower of drops.

Winter gazes at her, bewildered. She is almost a young woman. When did he grow so old?

"Come, Father." Spring skips ahead of him. In her wake, snow melts and grass grows.

"I told you, but you would not listen. Farewell." North Wind stirs the branches above and blows away. The air warms, and new flowers fill it with fragrance.

Winter walks ever slower until he reaches his garden, where Spring stands, weeping. "Our ice flowers are dying," she mourns.

He touches her shoulder with a hand that trembles. "Perhaps they shall live again one day, my child." Turning, he hobbles into the house.

Spring tucks him into bed and waits until he falls asleep. Then she kisses his forehead and smiles.

"Sleep well, Father," she whispers, and she shuts the door softly and runs out into the warm green morning.